SLOBCAT

Paul Geraghty

HUTCHINSON
London Sydney Auckland Johannesburg

For Harriet and the Moppets

First published in 1991
3 5 7 9 10 8 6 4 2
Paul Geraghty has asserted his right under
the Copyright, Designs and Patents Act, 1988
to be identified as the author of this work

First published in the United Kingdom in 1991 by
Hutchinson Children's Books
Random House UK Limited
20 Vauxhall Bridge Road, London SW1V 2SA

Random House Australia (Pty) Limited
20 Alfred Street, Milsons Point, Sydney,
New South Wales 2061, Australia

Random House New Zealand Limited
18 Poland Road, Glenfield
Auckland 10, New Zealand

Random House South Africa (Pty) Limited
PO Box 337, Bergvlei 2012, South Africa

Random House UK Limited Reg. No. 954009

A CIP catalogue record for this book
is available from the British Library

ISBN 0 09 174195 5

Printed and bound in Belgium by Proost

Slobcat is our cat.
He does nothing but lie
about and sleep.

Heaven knows what
he does when we're
not there.

But when we get home he's still sleeping. That's why we call him Slobcat.

When it's his dinner time,
he's nowhere to be seen...

…and when we *do* find him,
he's even too lazy to eat.

I don't know *where* he goes
when we put him out...

...but he often comes back
soaking wet because he's
too lazy to shelter from
the rain.

He spends so much
time inside...

...that he ends up getting in the way!

Last week Mum saw a mouse, so Dad put out a trap...

...because Slobcat
isn't interested
in chasing mice.

All *he's* interested in is lying about
in the sun.

Luckily,
we don't have rats...

…because if we did,
Dad says we'd have to
get a proper cat.

Some people have
dangerous animals
in their gardens.

But for some reason,
they don't seem to
come into ours.

It's strange because
the *little* creatures
don't seem afraid.

Sometimes, when we're asleep, there are burglars about.

Thank goodness
we have Brutus to
frighten them
off…

...because Slobcat couldn't
frighten a flea!

People say that all cats have a secret
life that we don't know about…

...but I'm sure Slobcat's much too lazy for that!